This novel is a work of fiction. Names, characters, places, events, and incidents are either products of the author's imagination or are used fictionally.

ISBN: 9798989636945

Published by Big Bricks Publications

Edited by Shawna Brim for Ladies of Lit

Cover design by Israr Khan

PROLOGUE

It took four rings before Cleon finally answered his phone, but I knew he would. He was my best friend and brother from another mother. Always dependable and ready to have my back, no matter the circumstance. Just last year, I had leaned on him to help me through some relationship drama, and now, here I am with yet another mess I'd gotten myself into. But there was no one else I'd confide in before turning to Cleon.

"Wow, that's crazy! I told you to stop fucking with them professional types," he gloated.

"Your luck any better with those hoeshas you date?"

"Say what you want but Hoesha ain't never had me laying up in the hospital or sitting in jail."

"Are you coming or not?" I conceded; his points were valid, but I wasn't in the mood to hear it.

"You know I got you," replied my loyal best friend.

"Thanks, bro! Try to get here as fast as you can."

As soon as I ended the call, I immediately realized I had messed up. You see, Cleon was down for me like A.C. was down with O.J., but his character flaw was being the worst at keeping a secret. I didn't want my personal business to become the newest barbershop gossip; however, I didn't instruct Cleon on what to do with what I just shared with him. By not emphasizing *'keep it to yourself'*, it somehow allowed him to believe that the information was free to share with anyone who'd listen. Even telling him not to say anything didn't guarantee that he would respect the code of confidentiality. So, more than likely, as soon as we hung up, Cleon, being the hood reporter that he was so passionately known to be, was entertaining everyone at Goodfellas Barbershop to the hot off the press breaking news.

"Mm mm mm... Y'all ain't gone believe this shit."

CHAPTER 1

"Good morning, Mrs. Ellis."

"Good morning to you, Brands."

Damn, that woman was gorgeous. The best part of my day was five minutes after nine. That was about the time Tralisha came bouncing her fine ass through the front door. Good thing I was seated behind this desk. She just caused my little big man to stand at attention, and that was not something I wanted her to see. Well, maybe I would, but not like this and certainly not here.

"I was dreading coming here today and dealing with these crazy people, but seeing your smiling face has already improved my mood."

Was she flirting with me? Nah, I had to be taking it the wrong way. Tralisha was usually high on professionalism and super low on personal interaction around the office. It took a few months of me being here before she'd even look in my direction for a simple exchange of pleasantries. Usually, it was just a head nod or hand wave while walking by, but she eventually warmed up to smiling at me and asking how I was doing.

For about the last month, Tralisha made it a point to walk over to my desk every day and spark up a conversation. It felt strange at first because this was new behavior from her, but I had to admit that our interaction felt really pleasant. She did most of the talking; I simply nodded and answered her questions to be polite. Over time, as we chatted more, I became increasingly open-minded about speaking freely around her.

"That must mean I'm good at doing my job," I proudly responded with a smile.

"Indeed, you are. But can you do me a favor?"

"Absolutely!"

"Mrs. Ellis is my mother. I loved her with all my heart, may she rest in peace, but I'm quite too young to be given that old lady's name."

"My bad. It wasn't my intention to offend you."

"No apologies needed, and no offense taken. I just don't want you to think of me as older or married. I'd rather you view me on equal terms and someone you could consider a friend."

Okay, it felt like she was flirting. I might have been misinterpreting this because I'd intentionally been out of touch with women lately. I began working as a security guard at the bank five months ago, and from the start, I had been having internal discussions with myself to ensure I stuck to the assignment. I was here to work, which meant keeping my focus on monitoring the entry doors and surveillance cameras. I could never again allow myself to get distracted or close to any woman in a way that could lead to a repeat of what happened last year with Sherie.

"I'm a bit old-fashioned when it comes to stuff like this, but would you like to hang out sometime?" Tralisha blurted out to my surprise.

"Come again?" I wanted to be sure I heard what I thought I heard.

"I'm taking it you were never going to ask, and there's just not enough free time in a workday for us to interact here at the bank and really get to know each other," she explained.

"I had no idea you were interested in getting to know me. I thought we were just chatting it up like coworkers do."

"Other than pop out a titty right here at your desk, I don't know how else I could've revealed that I'm fond of you. You've been sitting here at this desk, focused on work, for so long that you're forgetting to look up occasionally and see the sunshine."

"With what I've been through, keeping my head down and minding my business is the best thing for me."

"Sounds like there's a story to that. Maybe you can tell me all about it over dinner?"

I would've loved to quickly agree to her request, but I had a good and bad conscience that were constantly talking to me internally and liked to slow down my responses while they deliberated over my life's decisions:

"My guy, she is throwing us a big ass bone. You better speak up before we miss out," said Cameron, my bad conscience.

"I don't think that's a very good idea," Jonathan, my good conscience, said in disagreement.

"We know you wouldn't, square. Back off! This has nothing to do with you."

"This is the very definition of something that has everything to do with me. I'm always the one left to clean up the messes you made. It would behoove you to ignore Cameron on this one. Tell her it's nice that she offered but it's probably not a good idea to date a coworker," Jonathan pleaded.

"Not a good idea? This beautiful woman badly wants a piece of us, and her lips are talking directly to the dick. The only thing she mentioned was

hanging out with us. That's usually code for 'this pussy's yours if you want it.' Yeah, I see you looking, playboy. Go ahead, make our motherfucking day!" Cameron said, further stating his case.

"It feels like you're going to listen to this fool, but don't say I didn't warn you," Jonathan digressed.

Both sides made valid points. Given the workplace drama I'd been through just last year, a wise choice would be to decline. On the other hand, from just the small chitchats we had, Tralisha seemed like she'd be a cool person to get to know outside of work. We chopped it up like good friends and had a matching sense of humor. Sometimes, we would even finish each other's sentences.

To top it off, Tralisha was absolutely gorgeous. Didn't wear much makeup on her pretty chocolate face. The perfume she wore smelled delectable. Always walked into the bank dressed like money wasn't a thing. Last but not least – and I wouldn't act like I didn't know because I'd certainly been looking – she had the body of a Bad Mamma Jamma, just as fine as she could be.

By society's standards, Tralisha was considered a plus size woman. There was absolutely nothing wrong with that when the woman was big and had curves in all the right places. Tralisha had big breasts, thick thighs, and a fat, round ass that I adored. She wore it with pride too and loved to dress in a way that showed off the great body she possessed. When they looked as sexy and well put together as Tralisha did, I'd choose a BBW every time.

At this point, I liked everything I knew about Tralisha. Plus, she was not married, so I didn't have to worry about another man knocking on my door threatening me about his wife. She was not Sherie or Evette, but if I ever wanted to get back to living a normal life, I couldn't compare the new women that came about to anyone I'd dealt with in my past. Sometimes, the bad conscience and the little big man needed to come out and play. Choosing to do the wise thing could go fuck itself.

"I'd love to have dinner with you."

CHAPTER 2

"Hey, Brands," said Tralisha, entering the bank at her usual time.

"Good morning, pretty lady."

"You're so sweet. Thank you for the compliment! I actually needed to hear that because I sure don't feel like it right about now."

"You're welcome. Although it sounds like there's a story to that."

"There is. I'd say I'd tell you about it over dinner, but it doesn't seem like you are ever going to be available for that to happen."

My schedule made it challenging to coordinate dinner arrangements with Tralisha. There was a shortage of security officers and being relatively new in my role made me susceptible to working shifts that no one else wanted. Whenever my boss asked me to work extra hours, I didn't hesitate to accept because I wanted to be known as someone the bank could always depend on. Plus, the additional time and a half on my paycheck made it well worth it, and night shifts at the bank were easy money.

I was actually okay with the fact that right now my work schedule prevented me from hanging out with Tralisha. I went back-and-forth with the idea. Some days, I was excited about getting together with her, but then, there were moments when I feared following through with the date plans. Even though I agreed to it when Tralisha first asked, what happened to Sherie last year had me thinking that it might not be wise to travel down such a similar path yet again.

At the beginning of the murder investigation, I would phone Detective Bill Peters at the Chandler Police Department once or twice a week to find out what progress was being made with apprehending Darrell, Sherie's former husband and killer. Every week, the detective would have nothing to report. Wherever Darrell escaped to, he mastered how to stay hidden from the police, and it began to feel as if he would never be brought to justice.

Weeks turned into months, then several months, and before I knew it, a year had passed dealing with the police and their inability to solve the case. After every disappointing conversation with Detective Peters, I began to give up hope and checked in with him less often. Eventually, Sherie became less of a thought as well, so much so that I allowed myself to be open to the possibilities with Tralisha.

"I promise it will be any day now," I said, hoping to reassure Tralisha that I was definitely still interested.

"I'm holding you to that," Tralisha said playfully.

"You can take it to the bank."

"Now that was clever." She chuckled.

"It got you laughing, didn't it?"

"Yes, and I like that about you. It's refreshing and attractive that you can make me laugh and smile without much effort."

"Good morning, Miss Ellis," said Marvin, my boss, appearing suddenly as if from nowhere.

I met Marvin O'Neale last year at Goodfellas Barbershop. He had been the Regional Director of Security at Citizens First Bank for the past seventeen years, overseeing all of its retail branches across Arizona, California, and Nevada. He found himself needing to quickly hire a security officer for a branch located in Tempe, Arizona, and it was perfect timing for my situation being that I had recently lost my job as a sales agent.

Even though I didn't have any prior security experience, Marvin offered me the job right on the spot after several members of the barbershop family vouched for my professional character. Not wanting to be unemployed for too long, I quickly accepted, and since then, it felt like a blessing to work for him and learn a plethora of new things. It was not just about bank security, but he had also become an invaluable life mentor to me.

"Hey, Mr. Marvin! We haven't been graced with your presence in quite some time," said Tralisha, excitedly greeting him back.

"Thanks to all the good work this young man has been doing, there hasn't been much of a reason for me to come around," said Marvin, proudly complimenting the quality service I was providing to the bank.

"He's certainly been a wonderful addition to the team. I, for one, feel safer having him here. Well, I better get back to my desk and act like I work here. Take care, Mr. Marvin. I'll catch up with you later, Brands."

"Have a good day, Miss Ellis," I responded, using her surname around my boss, hoping it appeared that our interaction was purely professional.

"I see it didn't take too long for you to make yourself

comfortable around the ladies," joked Marvin.

"Oh, that was nothing. Just a brief good morning conversation."

"Tralisha has been here for three years, and I can't ever recall a time when she's made her way over to this desk to say '*good morning*' to any of my other officers."

"I bring out the best in people," I said playfully.

"Be sure that's the only thing you bring out. Fine young lady like that might make you forget the reason you're here."

CHAPTER 3

Night shifts at the bank were usually mundane. Once all of the office staff left at six o'clock, my job duties were to ensure all entry doors were secured and that the alarm system was activated. After that, the only task I had until six in the morning was to keep a watchful eye on the security cameras. Most nights, I was there alone, minus the few hours on Tuesdays and Fridays that the janitorial staff showed up to clean the building. The ultraquiet, dimly lit environment made it, at times, hard to stay awake, but two NoDoz tablets and a sixteen-ounce can of Red Bull had me so hyper caffeinated that there was no way in hell I could fall asleep, even if I wanted to.

A few hours into my shift, unexpectedly the buzzer for the rear door chimed through the computer speakers connected to the security system. This was bizarre because nothing was scheduled for maintenance or deliveries on this Thursday night. To my surprise, the video monitor displayed Tralisha standing at the entrance. She waved with her right hand and in her left hand held up to the camera what looked to be a restaurant food bag.

It was security protocol to never open any entry doors during lockdown hours, as this would trigger a silent alarm alerting law enforcement to an assumed breaking and entering or robbery in progress. The service entrance was the one exception. Its alarm was disabled while I was on the clock, and the camera footage was rarely reviewed because most all that would be seen was the comings and goings of night porters disposing of trash bags and recyclables.

In her role as a manager, Tralisha was one of the few bank employees who knew the procedure for the rear door. She knew it was the only door that she could get away with entering after business hours. Even still, in all of my months working here at the bank, there had never been a time until now that Tralisha showed up at the service entrance, especially at this time of night.

I made my way to the service door, perplexed as to why she was here at this late hour, but I had to admit I was also excited that she was here. I was taking a chance at losing my job letting her inside the building, but Tralisha was someone who I considered a good enough friend that I trusted her presence here would be harmless. She was also someone I was romantically attracted to, which definitely added to her being worth the risk. Plus, I was dying of boredom and, being a bit hungry, I was curious to know what she had waiting for me in that food bag.

"I never took you as a lady of the night," I said jokingly.

"Now is that the way to greet someone bringing you dinner?"

"Depends on what you brought."

"Only the best barbeque Phoenix has to offer," she bragged.

"Famous Dave's?"

"I'm pretty sure I said the best barbeque."

"How dare you bash Dave's like that," I contested.

"It can't touch any parts of what I got in this bag from Trap Haus BBQ," Tralisha rebutted.

"Alright. You can come on in, and I'll give it a try, but if it's not what you say it is, I'm putting your ass back out on the street."

When we made it back to my desk, Tralisha unbagged the food and fixed me a plate. There was beef brisket, potato salad, collard greens, black eyed peas, cornbread, some sweet potato pie for dessert, and a large container of sweet tea to wash it all down with. It looked and smelled delicious. The only thing left to do was to taste it all to confirm if Tralisha knew what she was talking about when she claimed that Trap Haus was the best barbeque in town.

"Better than Dave's," said Tralisha, not asking for my validation but rather asserting as if she was already certain I approved.

"You're still here, ain't you?" I licked the sauce from my fingers, then responded sarcastically; this being my way to quietly consent that Trap Haus was indeed better barbecue than Famous Dave's.

We continued to eat while talking for quite some time about our favorite activities. I discovered that just like me, Tralisha was a cinephile who frequented movie theaters once, or even twice, a week and loved all genres of cinema. We both loved camping, and karaoke, and were fans since childhood of World Wrestling Entertainment. In previous relationships, I often had to impose my interests on the other person. It was refreshing to finally feel like I had found someone who was ying to my yang.

I finally decided to ask Tralisha what she was doing here. She assumed with all the hours I was working it would be nearly impossible for us to find some time to hang out. Rather than wait until an opportunity presented itself, she decided to take matters into her own hands and visit me here at the bank where she knew I always was. She hoped I didn't take offense with her infringing on my personal and professional space. I communicated that although uninvited guests were the most irritating thing to me, I was glad that she was here, and it was very thoughtful of her to bring me food to eat.

"I've been enjoying your company so much I almost forgot that I'm on the clock and need to make my rounds," I said, hinting that it was time for her to go.

"If I promise not to be a distraction, can I stay and walk around with you?" Tralisha petitioned.

"It's not a very exciting task, but yeah, that's cool."

"Any time I get to spend with you is all the excitement I need."

Tralisha and I talked non-stop as we walked around the building. While I listened to her tell me about graduating from Indiana University, I was multitasking, turning knobs and tugging on handles to make sure that doors were properly secured. I didn't have much of a college story to share back, being that I'd dropped out after only taking a few business classes at the University of Phoenix. She was impressed when I mentioned that after high school, I traveled to all fifty states and several countries, performing with my band.

"How has it been transitioning to doing security work?"

"I actually went into sales first. Figured since I was good at convincing people to buy my music, it probably wouldn't be too difficult to sell them insurance."

"How did that go?" she inquired.

"I hated it, but I was a top performer, and the money was great."

"I'm sure you were the best salesperson the company had. You're already the best security officer at the bank. To hear that you've traveled all over doing the thing that you loved to do the most, it's a wonderful accomplishment that you should be proud of. I bet you're great at whatever you put your mind to."

Tralisha's compliments were satisfying to my soul. They made me feel warm inside and even aroused me. We were on the elevator, making our way to the highest level so that I could double check the rooftop perimeter. While the elevator climbed floors, I quickly stepped toward Tralisha then wrapped my arms around her, rubbing up and down across her back and pulling her in as close to my body as I possibly could. We were pressed up against each other so closely that I could feel her heart beating rapidly, and I was certain she could feel mine as well.

We began to kiss deeply. Our tongues wildly circled each other. Occasionally, I nibbled on her juicy bottom lip. Then, I forcefully spun her around so that the front of her body was pinned against the elevator wall. The front of me was now connected to the backside of her as I purposefully made sure that her soft, voluptuous ass could feel every inch of my rock-hard dick pressed against her.

She moaned intensely. Just as Tralisha turned back to face me, the elevator stopped escalating and then made a dinging sound, indicating that we'd made it to the top floor. While waiting for the doors to swing open, we came to our composure, attempting to settle down our breathing and fix our disheveled clothing.

CHAPTER 4

Now that Tralisha and I were on the roof, I scanned the premises for anything that looked abnormal or suspicious. I made a mental note of what time it was so that I could write it in my logbook when I returned to my desk. The scene was clear and incident-free as it usually was; there was never much patrolling to worry about when it came to this part of the building.

The entry point was the elevator, which required an access badge that only security officers and facilities managers were privy to. Other than the elevator, if someone wanted to get up or down from the roof, they would have to use the emergency escape ladder that scaled the entire fourteen floor building, which was heavily monitored with security cameras and motion sensors. Even still, despite the top level being low maintenance as far as my job was concerned, it was an important part of my job to inspect the roof level and all other checkpoints throughout the building every four hours of my overnight shift.

With work chores out of the way, now I could focus my attention on Tralisha. We walked to the back side of the rooftop where it overlooked an exquisite view of the Creator's sky above and the man-made Tempe Town Lake below. One of the perks that working the night shift provided me was that for the most part, I was in the building by myself. Occasionally, I took advantage of the idle time and would escape to the top floor for extended breaks, especially since no one would likely ever know what I was up to during my shift. The bank's building was the tallest in the area, so at this height, no one in the nearby structures could see me up here. I also discovered a section of the roof where the security cameras had no coverage. I took advantage of the situation and decided not to inform my boss, Marvin, so that I could secretly keep this location as a spot to relax or even take a nap from time to time.

The moon was exceptionally illuminated this evening, projecting its gorgeous light across the calm flow of the reservoir water. The moonlight beamed down upon Tralisha, showcasing her milk chocolate complected skin so perfectly. I imagined that if I tasted her, she would be as sweet and satisfying as a candy bar. Taking another long look at her, I was certain that Tralisha would be so gratifying to eat, and tasting every part of her, I intended to do. She stared at me with desire written all over her face. Being on this rooftop in seclusion, with the attraction we had for one another and the moon assisting with the ambiance, everything about this moment spewed romance and was the ideal setting for our first fuck.

Picking up where we left off in the elevator, I moved in close to Tralisha and passionately kissed her some more on the lips. Then, I pecked on her neck and chest. She softly moaned while lightly stroking my head. I began groping her breasts, then her plump ass. I grew impatient with the fabric covering her skin, and knowing that I didn't have much time to spend on foreplay given the fact that I was still on my work shift, I rushed to untie the drawstring on the Adidas sweatpants she was wearing and shimmied them along with her panties down and off her amazing thunder thighs and bubble butt.

I stepped back momentarily to gaze upon her gorgeous body. With the moon being our only light, the silhouette of her curvy, plus-size frame had my dick as hard as a metal pipe. Her naked flesh wore this seductive smell that had to be made up of the perfume she earlier sprayed across her chest and between her thighs mixed in with a subtle, naturally sweet release of endorphins, perspiration, and pussy juice. I inhaled deeply, and with just one whiff of Tralisha's body nectar, I was salivating and craving her as if I were Pepé Le Pew from the old *Looney Tunes* cartoon chasing after Penelope Pussycat.

"Remember earlier when you mentioned that I am probably great at whatever I put my mind to?"

"Yes, and I meant it," Tralisha said softly.

"Let me show you something else I am great at."

I instructed Tralisha to turn around and lean her body against the balcony fence. Then, I commanded that she spread her legs and reach around with her arms to hold open her ass cheeks. She looked back from behind with a raised eyebrow on her face, as if to express to me that we weren't yet on the kind of terms where I could be bossing her around like that; nevertheless, she did as she was told.

I got down on my knees and immediately used my tongue to taste every part of her vagina. I started off pleasuring her with slow, please-make-love-to-me licks, and then, I switched to giving her some fast-paced, aggressive, don't-fucking-stop-until-I-cum slurps. I used my tongue like it was a paint brush and licked her up, down, and side to side. Then, I used my tongue as if it was my dick and rapidly rammed it deep inside her pussy. I gave her the oral business as if I were a new hire on the job working harder than everyone else because I needed to make a good first impression. Her heavy breathing and legs trembling let me know that I was indeed putting in the kind of performance that would have her nominating me for employee of the month.

I munched on her pussy for several minutes more, doing everything I could with my mouth to make her have an orgasm that she would never forget. She pleaded for me to stop several times, letting me know that the sensation I was putting her body through was getting to be too much for her to handle. Every attempt she made to turn around and move my face from between her legs presented me with a challenge to lick her pussy even harder and faster to make her cum.

I closed my lips on her clit and sucked nonstop until Tralisha couldn't hold it in anymore. It felt like her whole body went into convulsions, and she did everything she could to keep her excitement and outbursts to a minimum. On the other hand, I did everything in my power to get even more orgasmic energy out of her. After a second round of convulsions, Tralisha's legs buckled, and her body collapsed to the bench seat. She was exhausted and could take no more of what I was giving her.

I lifted myself up from my knees and sat on the bench next to Tralisha. While pulling her panties up her right leg, she let out a long, drawn-out 'wow' as if to let me know that she was overwhelmingly impressed with what just took place.

"Thanks for dinner."

"You're welcome. When can I bring you dinner again?" Tralisha inquired.

"Whenever your heart desires. Just as long as I can have you for dessert."

CHAPTER 5

Over the next few months, it became a regular occurrence for Tralisha to visit me at the bank two or three nights a week. She always brought food, so we'd eat and then talk for a while. Afterward, while making my security rounds, we found some secluded spot in the building to have sex.

I was enjoying my time with Tralisha, and I could feel our interactions transitioning into an emotional connection. However, despite receiving from her a consistent, positive vibe and some of the best sex I'd had in a very long time, I could never forget the past, fatal mistake I made while dating a coworker. I had a conversation with Tralisha to make it clear that, currently, I was only interested in being friends.

She agreed that was probably the best situationship for us being that we worked together. Simultaneously, we blurted out excitedly that there was absolutely nothing wrong with being friends who fucked. We sealed the deal with a long, passionate kiss, then hurried to undress, and sealed the deal again having sex until we climaxed at the same time.

CHAPTER 6

Today was my birthday; the twenty-ninth flight around the world. Every year on this day when I woke up, the very first thing I did was meditate for thirty minutes or so. I used that time to talk to my Higher Power and to express gratitude for blessing me with a wonderful life and good health. Then, I usually spent the rest of my morning responding with heart emojis on social media posts from my family and friends wishing me well.

With my attention focused on my phone, I didn't notice that Tralisha was standing in front of me at my desk until she cleared her throat. She had a pissed-off look on her face that quickly took the happy-to-see-you smile off my face.

"Everything okay?" I inquired.

"Happy birthday," she said sarcastically.

"Thank you. Wait, how did you know it was my birthday?"

"Exactly! Why wasn't I informed of that information from you instead of by the rude woman that just walked in here with cake and balloons claiming to be your girlfriend?"

"Tralisha, lower your voice," I pleaded, scanning the lobby for anyone eavesdropping on our conversation.

"How could you leave me in the dark like that? I thought we had a good thing going on."

"Calm down. You're just taking this—"

"I know you just did not tell me to calm down!" She raised her voice, which echoed throughout the building, making it abundantly clear to those nearby that something was amiss between us.

"Stop it before one or both of us end up without a job. I will talk with you about this later," I whispered calmly through gritted teeth and pursed lips, concealing any emotion my face might be showing to onlookers.

"I'll do you one better. Unless it's work related, there's no reason for us to ever speak again," she blurted out with finality as she stormed off toward her office.

The up-tempo, clicky-clack of her heels marched away from me, playing an irate and disappointed sounding tune. It was not the sound of her walking away in shame as if it was the next morning after having sex with a man on the first night. This sound was more like a fuck-him-girl, men-ain't-shit jingle that resonated down the halls and didn't end until the thud of the office door she closed with force relieved me of the torturous noise. This was yet another fucked up situation I'd gotten myself into, and thinking about it now, with both Sherie and Tralisha, the root cause of it all had been the same – Evette!

"Why are you here?" I discreetly barked at Evette as soon as I entered the lobby waiting area where she was seated alone.

"Damn, I don't get a hello?" she insisted.

"Hello. What the fuck are you doing here?"

"Happy birthday! These are for you," she said, excited to hand over the gifts she'd brought me.

"Thank you. Is that it?"

Even though her purpose here was for a considerate gesture,

I disregarded the sentiment and was uninterested in any further interaction. I didn't hide my frustration with her assuming that it was okay to invade my place of business in this manner. I would've preferred she delivered these to my apartment, especially since she had no problem with popping up whenever she felt like it, even after knowing better than anyone else that I despised uninvited guests.

"Well, there is something else. I have some great news, and I thought it'd be better to surprise you with it in person," Evette said cheerfully.

"I could care less what you got going on. You are not my woman anymore, and now, thanks to your ass, I may have just lost my job. I need you to leave right now!" I commanded with authoritative bass coming from my voice.

"I promise you'll want to hear this."

"Evette, if you show your face here again, I promise to have you arrested for trespassing. Am I making myself clear?"

Her eyes began to water, and a single tear streamed down her left cheek. She turned her body toward the exit and nodded slightly to relay her understanding. I couldn't fathom why I would even care, but now, I felt bad for making her cry. After all the emotional bullshit this woman has put me through, I was still contemplating apologizing to someone who wronged me and didn't deserve an ounce of my compassion.

"Hold up a second," I called out just as Evette made contact with the push bar on the exit doors.

I consoled her by rubbing my hand across the back of her neck and shoulders while I walked her outside. I explained to her, as softly as I could, that although my anger and harsh words were warranted for showing up at my workplace and getting into an altercation with Tralisha, I knew that she meant well and only wanted to do something special for me on my birthday. Evette smiled brightly when I mentioned that now wasn't a good time, but I'd be in touch, so she could share with me whatever it was she wanted to talk about.

When I walked back into the bank, Tralisha was standing in the lobby not too far from the entry doors. Her hands were wrapped tightly across her chest, and her stern demeanor conveyed disappointment toward me. I didn't want another altercation to occur – given how loudly and inappropriately she last spoke to me in our professional environment – so I said nothing and walked past her heading back to my desk. I could have tried to ease any concerns Tralisha had about my status with Evette, but I was annoyed with her at the moment and decided whatever I had going on with Evette was no business of hers.

"I'll do it," Tralisha said privately into her iPhone.

CHAPTER 7

"I'm here to inspect the vault," said a man.

"Good morning to you too, sir," I replied sarcastically, irritated by him barking demands without first acknowledging my awesome existence.

"Forgive me if I don't have time for small talk. I have another inspection across town to get done within the hour."

"No one told me about this. You'll need to wait over there while I check into it," I barked back, not giving him eye contact while pointing to the lobby waiting room.

"How about letting me start doing my job while I'm waiting for you to do yours?"

"Because that's not how we do business around these parts."

"I have serviced every bank in the Valley for the last decade, and no one has ever wasted my time with this like you're doing right now."

"Doesn't matter to me what everyone else does. I don't know you, bro. No one told me you were coming, so have a seat or feel free to leave," I responded with a strengthened tone and gave the man a look that implied knuck-if-you-buck.

"Excuse me, Brands," Tralisha intercepted what was turning into a cheeky exchange between two alpha males.

I was shocked at her presence because it had been a couple of weeks since she last spoke to me. Every morning, she walked into the bank and right past me without even a glance in my direction. I found it immature and unprofessional, but it is what it is. I was here to do a job, and going forward, that was exactly what I intended to do. I only wished that I'd never let my guard down and gotten romantically involved with Tralisha because now I had to try my best to coexist with her in what had seemingly become a hostile work environment.

"Yes, Tralisha. How can I help you?"

"I was walking by and couldn't help but overhear what was going on."

"You know this guy?" I inquired.

"Yes, his name is Thomas. He is who he says he is."

"Then why is there no mention of any inspection on the schedule?"

"That's because it happens at random. If you check the certificate hanging in the vault, then you'll see that it's usually around this time of the year," she clarified.

"I don't like this guy's attitude, but since you're a manager, if you approve his entering the vault, that works for me."

"Yes, I approve."

I waved Thomas over to sign the visitor's logbook and to receive an ID badge to clip on his shirt. I then directed him to stand against the white wall so that per regulation, I could snap a picture of him. Thomas wasn't very tall for a man. My guess was five-foot-seven, and soaking wet looked to weigh a buck fifty or so. He had dark skin, long, thick dreadlocks, and was wearing blue jean overalls with a plain white t-shirt underneath and tan Timberland boots.

I didn't notice until now that there was a teardrop tattoo under his right eye. Usually, the only reason someone got brandished with one of those on their face was to signify they'd committed a murder. Then again, he could've been some clown assuming it was okay to mark his body with that horrific, tasteless symbol to make a fashion statement; something told me this dude was the latter. I chuckled under my breath then handed him the badge so that he could complete the inspection and get his phony ass out of my bank as soon as possible. I wished Tralisha hadn't come over to save the day because I wouldn't mind being a bigger asshole than him and sending this dude on his way not able to do the job he came to do.

I must say that Tralisha looked stunningly beautiful when she popped up at my desk. She was wearing a sleeveless, black, knee-length dress paired with a white waist belt and leopard print ankle boots. The dress hugged every part of her body, and the top exposed the perfect amount of titty meat that could entice a millionaire male executive into transferring all of his bank accounts over to this branch – maybe even a few lady bosses too – but it was still a professional, non-slutty ensemble that was within the dress code deemed appropriate by corporate policy.

Right then, I imagined storming into her office, locking the door, and shutting the blinds. I would step into her personal space and begin kissing her lips and neck. Next, I would cause everything on her desk to come crashing down on the floor, lay her back across it, run my hand up her dress to grab a fistful of her panties, and then rip them away from her lady parts. I'd unbuckle and unzip my work slacks to let them fall to my knees, release my dick from my boxers, spit into my right hand, and stroke the resting little homie, Bruce Banner, until it transformed into the enormous, ultra-excited Incredible Hulk I needed him to be for those special occasions. Once I rammed my superhero inside her, it wouldn't take long before the both of us were shaking from an orgasm and out of breath.

"What will it take for you to learn that some things are better left alone?" Jonathan lectured me about my impure thinking.

"Hurts me to agree with Goody Two-Shoes, but there's too many fish in the sea to keep casting your line at this same dame. Don't fuck around and find out," urged Cameron.

The fellas were right, plus Marvin already gave me a warning that I could lose my job if I let my personal life interfere with my professional expectations at the workplace. I quickly instructed the Hulk to shrivel back into Bruce, and I took my lustful thoughts off of Tralisha. Neither she nor any other woman was worth fucking up my money because I couldn't keep my dick in my pants.

CHAPTER 8

"You can't be here," I said firmly.

Tralisha pierced me with a no-the-fuck-you-didn't look, baffled that I was stopping her from entering the back door of the bank. During our last encounter about a month ago, she harshly expressed that we never needed to speak again. Well, I chose to honor that request, and since these late-night hours weren't her shift, her presence here could jeopardize my employment. It wasn't just my good conscience, Jonathan, screaming at me internally not to be stupid about this; now, my boss, Marvin's recent advice was also playing through my mind:

"I told you not to get involved with that young lady," Marvin lectured after receiving word from Human Resources about what occurred between Tralisha and me.

"My bad for stepping out of line. I assure you it'll never happen again."

"I know it won't. You've been nothing but responsible and hardworking, which is why I convinced corporate not to let you go. Besides, it's not like I haven't allowed a skirt to cloud my judgment when I sat in that very same chair."

"What happened, Mr. Marvin?" My inquiring, nosey mind wanted to know.

"It was long ago, and I don't care to relive any part of it. Bottom line is, it ended my marriage. I lost a good woman, but I'm blessed to still have my job and that I can stand here as a testament and warning to you that this is not the place to look for love."

"I hear you loud and clear, and sorry that happened to you," I empathized.

"Don't feel sorry for me, young brother. Just do better!" Marvin concluded.

"I'm probably not your favorite person right now, but I'm hoping we can share a meal and talk through some things," said Tralisha.

She looked so damn delicious that whatever she had in that food bag wasn't the only thing I wanted to eat. Her shoulder-length dreadlocks were styled in a ponytail flowing down the right side of her face, slightly covering her almond shaped, beautiful, brown eye and dimpled, chubby cheek. She had on a white, strapless, corset top paired with a tight fitting, denim miniskirt and two-inch, snake print, leather heels. Her enormous breasts protruded from the corset, and all of her exposed flesh appeared to have been lathered with glittery lotion that made her look smooth and sparkly.

"I can't have you on the premises like this. I'm lucky to still have a job," I barked.

"I'm so sorry about that, Brands. I promise you nothing like that will ever happen again. Please give me thirty minutes so I can explain why I reacted like that?"

The soft, soothing tone of Tralisha's voice, combined with her perfect beauty, made my dick hard. It was now more difficult for me to stand firm with the situation. I could hear Marvin and Jonathan's voices growing louder in my head, urging me to '*just do better,*' while Cameron, always the mischievous one, tussled with them both to be the voice of reason I ultimately surrendered to. Marvin and the corporate folks at Citizens First Bank had entrusted me with making intelligent decisions to ensure the safety of the people and property I was here to protect. Today, I would choose to do the right thing by following bank protocol, as I always should. But then, I thought of a way for me to have my cake and eat it too.

"Look, Tralisha, you can't be here right now, but how about you come by my place instead?"

"I really would like to spend time with you now."

"Take it or leave it."

"Guess I have no choice but to take it," she pouted, sounding defeated.

Tralisha handed me the bag of food, and I thanked her generosity with a close, long, squeezing hug. After just one whiff of the fragrance coming from her neck, I was ready to renege on not allowing her to enter the bank. I knew from firsthand experience that her pussy tasted just as wonderful as the pleasant smell she sprayed on her skin. We stared deeply at each other for a moment and then passionately kissed. Tralisha put two of my fingers in her mouth then eased them into her miniskirt where I soon discovered that she wasn't wearing any panties and that her wet clit was standing at attention just like my dick.

Once again, Marvin's voice echoed, reiterating that encounters like this should never happen at the workplace. I decided to obey, although both my dick and Cameron were displeased. She asked what time would be convenient to arrive at my apartment, and I gave her a few options. I thanked her again for bringing me dinner—and also for looking and smelling so damn good. With a playful twirl,

Tralisha showcased her amazing body, making it clear that every angle of her was equally stunning. At that moment, my resolve wavered, torn between duty and desire. I knew insisting she leave was the right choice, and as the saying goes, I sure did love to watch her walk away.

CHAPTER 9

It was around three in the afternoon on Saturday when I finally woke up from working the graveyard shift last night. I felt refreshed and ready to enjoy the rare occasion of having two work-free days in a row. With nothing on the agenda, I decided to spend some time doing house chores.

One thing that I loved to do while cleaning the apartment was sing along to country music. However, my predominantly Black neighbors weren't as enthusiastic about my musical choices. They would have preferred the windows to rattle and the walls thump with the sounds of rap or rhythm and blues.

The notification on my iPhone interrupted the music, alerting me that someone was ringing my doorbell. I didn't bother checking the security camera on the Wyze app to see who was at the door because, about thirty minutes earlier, I had placed an online order with Venezia's New York Style Pizzeria, so it was likely that my pizza and wings had arrived. When I opened the door, to my surprise, it was Tralisha standing at my front entrance.

We exchanged greetings, though mine were noticeably less excited. She was well aware that I wasn't a fan of unannounced guests, and sensing my annoyance, she apologized for the intrusion but defended herself by claiming she sent me a text about an hour ago.

That was when I remembered that when I started cleaning my house, I purposely ignored any notifications that came in so that I could focus on the task at hand, and during that time, I never checked for missed calls or messages. I still felt like she should have waited for my response before just popping up – someone could've already been here or I had plans to go out – but since I had nothing going on and she was already here, I welcomed her inside.

We weren't able to embrace just yet because she was holding my delivery order in her hands. She mentioned that both she and the driver arrived at the same time, so she accepted it for me and gave him a $10 tip. I placed the food on the table and thanked her with a big hug and a series of quick kisses, then I directed her to have a seat on the living room couch while I grabbed some napkins and Dasani water bottles from the kitchen.

During the meal, we made small talk about how this summer seemed hotter than the one before, but once we finished eating, the conversation shifted to the scandalous event that happened at work. I criticized her for assuming Evette was my girlfriend and that if she had given me a chance to explain, she would have discovered there was nothing to worry about. Tralisha didn't make any excuses; she simply apologized and asked for my forgiveness.

"Oh, I already forgave you. I like you too much to hold a grudge," I said with a soft smile.

"I like you a lot too. Actually, I think I love you, Brands," she declared.

"You think or you know?" I asked, attempting to hide from her my shock of what she'd just revealed.

"That depends. Am I someone you could love?"

"I'd like it if your feelings for me were your own and not based on how I feel about you."

"They are my own, but I also want to know what's going on in your head."

"It's ironic that now you want to know what's going on first," I said sarcastically.

"I'll never be able to live that down, will I?"

"Hey, I can forgive, but I didn't say I'd forget."

It was nice that we were now able to laugh and tease each other about the whole situation. I honestly did forgive her, and though I may never choose to let her know, I could also forget about it ever happening. Water under the bridge as far as I was concerned.

I realized then that I really missed not speaking to Tralisha over this past month. Getting back to normal with her felt satisfying to my soul, similar to when we had our first conversation at the bank. I had more than just "like" for her; she was beginning to mean more to me than Evette or Sherie ever did.

"Yes, Tralisha."

"Yes, what?"

"You are someone I could love."

Tralisha smiled from ear to ear, then suddenly tears trickled down her cheeks. I opened my arms for her to fall into them and held her for quite some time. Occasionally, I kissed her forehead and whispered that everything with us was going to be okay. We changed positions to lying cuddled on the couch. I reached for the remote on the coffee table in front of us and turned on the television to watch *The Walking Dead.* Tralisha fell asleep before the first episode of season one ended; her light growl of a snore rumbled across my chest. One episode later, I was asleep as well.

CHAPTER 10

I was jolted awake by an alert that came blaring from my iPhone on the coffee table. Squinting against the bright screen in the pitch-black living room, I was able to make out that I had some texts, emails, and social media posts to review. My attention was diverted to a notification from the Wyze app from a couple hours ago that read:

FRONT DOOR MOTION DETECTED 12:53 A.M. TAP TO REVIEW IT.

I realized then that Tralisha was no longer lying next to me on the couch. I tapped on the phone notification to view the camera recording, assuming it would show her departing. Sure enough, the footage captured her quietly closing the door and tiptoeing away from my apartment like a thief in the night.

Suddenly, another notification appeared. This time, it was a text from Tralisha that read:

I'm so sorry, Brands. You're a really good guy, and I hate that something like this had to happen to you.

Confused, I replied:

What does that mean?

Since we both had iPhones, the read receipt showed she'd viewed my message almost instantly, and the blinking ellipsis indicated she was typing a response. But after a few seconds, the dots disappeared, and no reply came through. Rather than wait, I decided to call. After just one ring, her voicemail greeting played.

"I hope everything is okay. Hit me back so I know what's going on."

I tried texting again, hoping for a quick reply. She didn't text back, so I called once more, but this time, it went straight to voicemail without even ringing. This wasn't like Tralisha; she'd always been super responsive. Whatever was going on, her actions made it clear that right now, she didn't want to be bothered.

Did she have a man this whole time? Had she gotten into it with him after leaving my place at such a late hour, and that was why she wasn't answering? My thoughts and emotions were all over the place, reminiscent of the discomfort I felt when I discovered Sherie had a husband.

"Fuck that! You are not getting bent all out of shape and end up a side piece to this chick like you were with Sherie," demanded Cameron.

"For once, I have to agree with Cam. Wash your hands of this situation before something stupid happens," Jonathan added.

"I must be right if this dude is siding with me."

"This isn't about which of us is right or wrong. This is about keeping Miles out of harm's way."

"Yeah, I know, but it still feels good to win one over you."

"Win what, Cam? See, that's the thing. You're always playing games, and then I have to step in and clean up your mess," Jonathan complained.

They were both right. Tralisha didn't deserve this much of my thoughts and energy, but still, she had it. I only intended for us to be close friends who, on occasion, were able to physically benefit from our personal and professional bond. Somehow, it didn't take long for

Tralisha to peel back my hardened, emotional layers and for my soul to be happy again. In her own way, without knowing it, she helped me heal from the pain I carried after Sherie's passing. So, I felt Tralisha was owed the benefit of the doubt. What if she had an emergency? What if something beyond her control was preventing her from answering my call? Before I assumed the worst, I needed to be sure, so I decided to call one last time. If she didn't answer, then I'd wash my hands of her.

Just as I dialed her number, I received a call from my boss. I was baffled by it – why would Marvin call at this hour, especially when I wasn't scheduled to work? I hesitated to answer, assuming he'd ask me to cover a shift. Knowing that I'd say yes, I thought it best to avoid him than to sacrifice a rare chance of enjoying two consecutive days off. But I couldn't ignore it. If Marvin was calling at three in the morning, it was for a good reason.

"Yes, sir." I altered my voice, pretending as if I was waking from sleep.

"I told you to leave that woman alone. I tried to help you, but you just couldn't listen and keep your dick in your pants. There's nothing I can do to save you from what comes next," he yelled.

"Whoa, Marvin, calm down! You're going to give yourself a heart attack, old man. Give me a chance to explain."

"Oh, soon enough, you'll have plenty of time to explain. Legally, I shouldn't even be calling, but I love you like a son, so I thought I should warn you."

"Warn me about wh–?"

Before I could finish my question, a loud crashing bang echoed through the front door of my apartment. Within seconds, a stampede of police officers burst in. Their weapons pointed, they yelled for me to not move, get on my knees, and put my hands above my head. Amidst the chaotic police commands, I could also hear Jonathan and Cameron pleading with me not to make any sudden moves and do exactly as I was told. I was shocked and clueless about what was happening, but according to Marvin, this ordeal had something to do with Tralisha.

CHAPTER 11

I was taken to the police precinct and interrogated for two grueling hours. The detective assigned to the case, a stern woman with piercing eyes, informed me that a burglary had occurred at the bank earlier that morning. She relentlessly peppered me with questions about my whereabouts and my connection to Tralisha. Although the detective wouldn't disclose all the details of her ongoing investigation, from the bits and pieces she did reveal, I learned that Tralisha was in custody, and an unidentified man had been killed at the scene.

The detective suspected I was involved because my ID badge was logged as entering the bank at an unauthorized hour. What neither I, Tralisha, nor any other branch-level employee knew was that, despite my badge having access to unlock doors and disable the alarm during my scheduled shift times, there were extra security measures in place that only a few entities were made privy to – the alarm system vendor, law enforcement, and Marvin, in his role as the Director of Bank Security. So, when my badge was swiped on the service entrance door panel at 2:07 a.m. in the back of the bank, it triggered a silent alarm, unbeknownst to Tralisha and her accomplice. Within ninety seconds, police officers were dispatched to the bank, and in under five minutes, they arrived on the scene to derail the burglary attempt.

I insisted to the detective that I had no knowledge of the burglary. With nothing to hide, I waived my right to speak with an attorney, fully cooperating by answering every question and sharing everything I knew about Tralisha. I revealed that we were intimately involved, that I loved her and believed she loved me back. We had spent yesterday at my apartment from around four in the afternoon until she left sometime after midnight while I was asleep. To prove my timeline, I showed the detective the saved recordings on my iPhone. I also shared the oddly worded text messages from Tralisha, where she apologized for what I now realize was her stealing my ID badge to access the bank. This evidence, combined with the bank's security camera footage, strongly supported my alibi.

The detective relentlessly interrogated me, mentally draining every ounce of my energy as she dissected every moment of the past twelve hours. She demanded an explanation for how my badge was used in the felony, suggesting that my role might have been to provide the badge in exchange for a share of the stolen goods. She questioned whether my feelings for Tralisha led me to protect her. Her warning that I could still be charged with aiding and abetting filled me with anxiety. Despite the intense pressure, I remained steadfast, assuring the detective that I had done nothing wrong.

Suddenly, a knock on the one-way mirror interrupted the detective, prompting her to excuse herself from the interrogation room. I was thankful for the invisible person on the other side of the window that rescued me from the overwhelming dialogue. Only then did I realize the throbbing headache that had taken hold, likely a result of the mental and physical strain from the relentless questioning during hours I would usually be counting sheep and calling hogs. The official police business had pushed my body to its limits, leaving me drained and disoriented.

With the detective gone, I had a moment alone to think about the scandal Tralisha had gotten me involved in. My mood shifted from shock to anger and then to sadness as I realized that this whole time, Tralisha had been playing with my emotions. It was hard to believe her true intention was to deceive me, all in an effort to commit a crime. She was a damn good con artist because the acting job she performed made me feel like she was genuinely into me and that we could end up in a relationship. I never thought I'd give in to loving someone like that ever again, especially after discovering Evette's infidelity and with what happened to Sherie. Tralisha changed my mind, opened my eyes, and made it easy to love again, but now, I knew that it was all a lie.

When the detective returned to the interrogation room, she announced that Tralisha had confessed to taking my badge without my knowledge. Then, I was shown a photograph and asked if I recognized the unidentified man the police killed earlier. I was shocked, staring at the photo of Thomas, who I had encountered a couple of weeks back when he visited the bank for a service inspection and who Tralisha had vouched for and authorized his access to the vault. She revealed to the detectives that Thomas was actually there to pinpoint what loot they wanted to steal, so they could get in and out quickly on the day of the burglary. However, their plan was derailed when Tralisha's eight-digit keycode failed to open the vault. She had no clue that there were security protocols in place, similar to my badge, that disabled her keycode permissions during non-working hours.

As police arrived outside the bank, Thomas became frantic

upon realizing there was no way to escape. He decided that he would not allow himself to be captured or go back to jail. The only way out of this predicament was to go out with a bang. The detective shared that the deceased, Thomas Harold Jones, had an arrest warrant in Indiana for a bank robbery that occurred last year along with an extensive rap sheet dating back to his childhood. According to Tralisha, had things gone as planned, she and her fiancé would have crossed the border to start a new life in Colima, Mexico.

"Fiancé?" I asked, seeking clarification.

"Count it as a blessing, Mr. Brandston."

"What's supposed to be the lesson in this?" I sarcastically questioned the detective.

"You're cleared of any wrongdoing, and you've been freed from fake love. Sounds like a guardian angel to me."

CHAPTER 12

"There's mail for you on the coffee table that just arrived."

"Thanks," I said while kissing Evette on her right cheek and giving her a playful slap on the ass as she went by me in the hall.

Six months had passed since I'd been fired from the security job at the bank. My former boss, Marvin, did everything he could to plead with the corporate office, but in the end, it was better for their reputation with shareholders and the public to relieve me from my post. Per the employee handbook, security personnel had an obligation to refrain from personal relationships with colleagues and customers. What happened with Tralisha and me was enough proof in the pudding as to why mixing business with pleasure never made sense. Add damage to company property and loss of life on the premises – let's just say I got what I deserved.

I hadn't yet obtained new employment, so unfortunately, I quickly burned through my savings, and the small amount I was receiving from unemployment could not adequately pay all of my monthly bills. This was the same scenario for Evette – ever since she resigned from her employment last year – so to make ends meet, we thought it'd be helpful to live together again. I wasn't interested in reuniting as a couple, something she bothered me with every damn day, but there was enough camaraderie between us to become roommates in an effort to save money.

Although I didn't want her as my lady, I found it extremely hard to physically resist Evette. It took less than a month of her walking around the apartment looking and smelling sexy for us to fall back into old habits, enjoying each other's company in ways that were familiar and comforting. Once we started having sex again, it became a regular occurrence. After every fuck session, Evette would annoyingly ask if we were getting back together. Each time, I would always respond that with everything that had happened to me over the past couple of years as it pertained to women, platonic sex was all I was interested in. Despite our different desires for our relationship status, our situationship functioned effectively and served its purpose well – at least that was how I saw it.

When I made it to the coffee table to retrieve the day's mail, the first thing I noticed stamped on one of the envelopes in the bottom left corner were bright red capital letters that read:

THIS MAIL IS FROM AN INMATE AT A STATE CORRECTIONAL INSTITUTION

I was bewildered after reading the cursive handwriting of an inmate from the Arizona State Prison Complex–Perryville, the sender being Tralisha Ellis, Inmate 393782. The salutation she used to address me was simply, *'Dear Miles'*, and she used the first sentence to inquire about my well-being. After that, she went on to apologize for what occurred, for lying to me, for damaging my professional reputation, and, if it so applied, for breaking my heart. She confessed that she still loved me and thought about me all the time.

I rolled my eyes and chuckled to myself as I continued to read her letter. My thoughts were that this was part of her prison rehab, her attempt to make amends with someone she hurt, but I was not interested in providing her with forgiveness. Despite needing to move on with my life, I was still angry, disappointed, and disgusted with her. She had made me lower my guard and open up my emotions to the idea of loving her, then she ripped the heart from my chest and spit a big loogie in my face. I was not sure I could ever forgive her or forget how she betrayed me.

In the last sentence, Tralisha mentioned that when she was done serving her seven-year sentence, she hoped that I would allow her to bring me a bag of dinner for old times' sake. She asked if we could sit and talk for hours and then find a rooftop so that I could make sweet love to her once again like I did on our first time. She ended the letter, *'Always Will, Tralisha'.*

That last line made me a little sentimental. That was a good day—a great day—one of the most romantic moments I'd ever shared with a woman. It wasn't long after that I could feel myself loving her. I was so giddy and in love with that woman that despite how corny the saying went I would've drunk her bath water. It was all ruined now. Regardless of anything wonderful we once had going on I couldn't see myself ever again wanting Tralisha like I did in the past.

I walked over to the fireplace and used the mantle to strike a match. Without hesitation, I began to burn Tralisha's letter then tossed it into the pit. As the ashes shriveled up in smoke and flew up the chimney, so did any leftover love I may have had for Tralisha. Time to move on to a new me, find some new work, and anything else new that I may need to get over the old things holding me hostage.

EPILOGUE

I was nervous sitting across the conference table from Joe Conover, the hiring manager at an extended-stay hotel, being interviewed for a night clerk position. My legs were shaking rapidly under the table as I was anxious to find out if this would be the day I'd finally be hired after not working for nearly a year. I had only a few hundred dollars in the bank, my emergency savings were depleted, and, though I appreciated her generosity, I didn't like the fact that for the last four months, Evette was covering all the living expenses.

This was probably the fifteenth interview I'd been on. I'd admit, most of the reason I was still jobless was because I had a bit too much pride about what kind of employment I would accept. Unfortunately, with my money now being a goddamn joke, I was no longer at liberty to be choosy about where I'd work next, so now I was desperate for any job I could receive. If I didn't leave this interview today with a start date, I'd be taking my broke ass to Taco Bell where they were currently having a same day hiring event.

"Marvin speaks highly of you," said Mr. Conover.

Despite what happened at the bank, Marvin remained a good friend and mentor, and there were no hard feelings between us. He stayed in touch by phone, and once or twice a month, I'd get to see him while hanging out with Cleon and the rest of my barbershop family at Goodfellas. Thanks to Marvin putting in a good word, I was blessed to meet with one of his fraternity brothers about a job opening.

"Working for Mr. O'Neale was invaluable and character-shaping for me. My attention to detail and communication skills are enhanced, as well as my ability to learn quickly, and being dependable and trustworthy. Thanks in large part to him taking me under his wing," I responded confidently.

"You mention trust. That will be extremely vital in this role. Marvin advised me of the trouble you got yourself into, and to be honest, if it wasn't for my fellow Que Dog calling in a favor, you wouldn't be sitting here."

I felt as if another job rejection was soon coming my way. I badly wanted to lower my head and pout in defeat, but I continued to make eye contact with Mr. Conover while anticipating his heartbreaking verdict. I hated that I would be forever hindered because of my role in what happened at the bank. It was inevitable that no major corporation would be interested in hiring someone who not one but twice had to be relieved of his duties due to what could be summed up as sexual misconduct at a place of business. I zoned out from listening to Mr. Conover as I mentally prepared myself for most likely becoming the newest crew member at a fast-food restaurant.

"Did you hear what I said, Miles?"

"Sorry, Mr. Conover. Could you repeat that please?"

"I said the job is yours, but on a provisional basis. One misstep of any kind and I'll have to let you go."

"Thank you so much, Mr. Conover. I promise I won't let you down," I responded excitedly and gave him a firm handshake.

We spoke for twenty minutes more about my work duties,

start date, pay, and what legal documents I needed to complete. Then, I was given a tour of the entire hotel and introduced to my new coworkers. My first impression of everything related to the hotel was pleasant. Although this was not what I envisioned I'd be doing for work, I had a feeling that it'd be a really cool environment to earn a paycheck.

When my meeting with Joe concluded, I made my way out of the front entrance of the hotel. My hands full with uniforms and new hire paperwork and my thoughts somewhere in the clouds, I failed to pay attention to where I was walking. I rounded the corner too tightly and accidentally bumped into someone making their way into the building, causing both of our belongings to fall to the ground. I apologized several times while kneeling to pick up all of the items. The sweet sound of a woman's voice caught me off guard. She seemed unfazed by the spill as she helped gather the scattered items.

"First day, huh?" she asked, an amused glint in her eyes. I laughed nervously, nodding.

"Long time coming." I exhaled then smiled.

"This is a nice place you'll be working, and I'm sure after some time on the job, you'll be less likely to bump into people," she joked.

"Sorry about that," I apologized again with an embarrassed tone.

"Oh, I'm just kidding with you. It's quite alright. I'm Deneen, by the way," said the beautiful woman, extending a hand.

"Nice to meet you. I'm Brands," I replied while taking her hand into mine.

"Your momma named you that?" she quipped.

"No, it's what I prefer my friends to call me."

"Since we're not friends, what name should a business customer refer to you as?"

"It's Miles." I altered my tone to a more appropriate corporate demeanor given that she changed the vibe of our interaction.

"Now that is the name of a handsome, distinguished gentleman. From what I see standing in front of me, it fits you way better than that neighborhood nickname," teased Deneen.

"Thank you. Well, if I ever get the chance to talk with you again, I give you the okay to call me whichever one you'd like. It was nice meeting you, Deneen. Enjoy the rest of your day."

I began walking toward the parking lot, wanting to end things with Deneen before I said anything to make a fool of myself. As I made my way to my car, for the first time in months, I felt like I was able to remove the weight of my burdens. This new job gave me a glimmer of hope. It was something noteworthy to light up the path ahead. Despite everything I'd been through, and every bad decision I'd made, the universe had given me another chance to get things back to where they needed to be.

"It was nice to meet you too – Brands!" Deneen yelled brightly.

I turned back in her direction and waved goodbye. As she walked through the entrance doors of the hotel, I was stunned to notice for the first time the impressive booty she wagged in behind her. I squinted my eyes to zoom in as best I could to stare at her derriere until it faded out of view.

Internally, Jonathan and Cameron were having a difference of opinion about my encounter with Deneen. I had to agree a little with Cameron that her referring to me as Brands was a hint of some sort, especially after she made it a point to let me know that we were not friends. I'd let the fellas sort things out, and they could fill me in later as to what conclusion they'd come to. It was 3:17 p.m., and the drive home would take me about twenty minutes. I needed to get some sleep so that I would be well rested for my first shift that was starting tonight at ten o'clock.

MORE TO COME

DID YOU ENJOY READING THIS BOOK?

Please help others enjoy it too.

Review it.
Recommend it.
Buy it for a friend.
Lend it.

Send me a message so that I can personally thank you by visiting the website: AndreBriscoe.com

OTHER RELEASES FROM BIG BRICKS PUBLICATIONS:

Bound By His Love

by Aleya Mishell

Misplaced Affections

by Aleya Mishell

Sins of My Brother

by Aleya Mishell

Conflicted

by Aleya Mishell

Conflicted 2

by Aleya Mishell

Casual Encounters With Women From Work (Book 1)

by Andre Briscoe

www.ingramcontent.com/pod-product-compliance
Lightning Source LLC
LaVergne TN
LVHW010944110826
845149LV00013B/2746

* 9 7 9 8 9 8 9 6 3 6 9 4 5 *